To my patient husband, Nick, my biggest fan and greatest confidante.

To my determined little boy, Palmer, who reminds me to be brave and follow my heart. You are my life's inspiration.

To my supportive parents. Thank you for raising us to be kind and accept people's differences, because at least you learn something, and at best, you make a new friend.

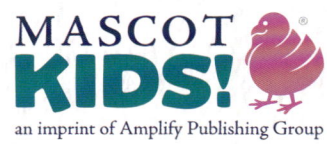

www.mascotbooks.com

Izzy and **Rubes** Practice Kindness

©2023 Marlaina Mannella. All Rights Reserved. No part of this publication may be reproduced, stored in a retrieval system or transmitted in any form by any means electronic, mechanical, or photocopying, recording or otherwise without the permission of the author.

For more information, please contact:
Mascot Kids, an imprint of Amplify Publishing Group
620 Herndon Parkway #220
Herndon, VA 20170
info@mascotbooks.com

CPSIA Code: PRKF0323A
Library of Congress Control Number: 2023902096
ISBN-13: 978-1-63755-774-7

Printed in China

Izzy and Rubes
Practice Kindness

Marlaina Mannella

Illustrated by
Tatiana Ross

There was a dazzling octopus named Izzy.
She owned a famous restaurant called Pop Fizzy's.
It was a grand place to eat made of coral,
decorated with algae and exquisite sea florals.

Izzy had three big hearts
and was exceptionally kind,
which explained why she helped others,
especially those in a bind.

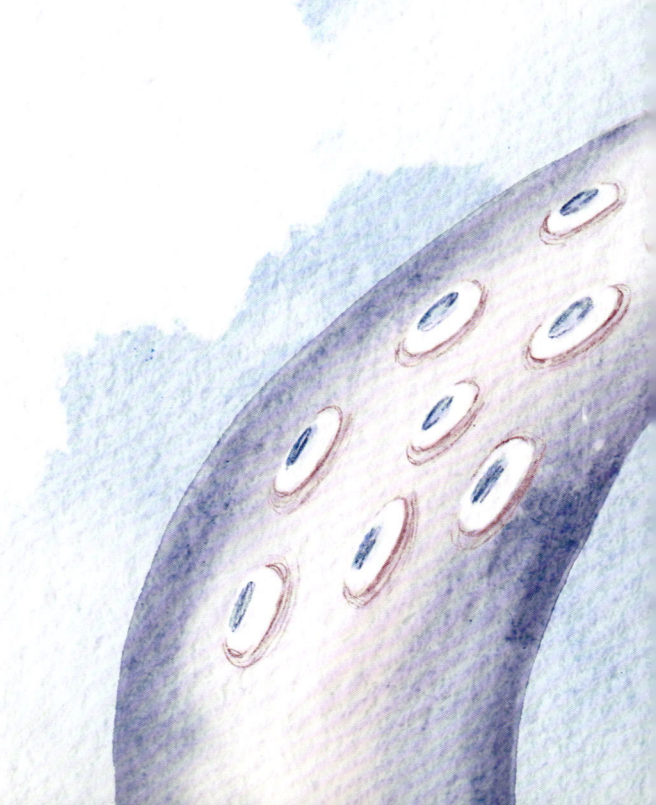

She loved her family a whole lot
and was a remarkable cook.
She spent time with her grandbabies
and loved to sing and read them books.

Every Saturday night Izzy would host a band,
and Pop Fizzy's watering hole filled with enthusiastic fans.
One evening, she signed a brand-new group.
The Jazzy Conch Fritters marched in like a musical troop.

The lead guitarist was a sea turtle named Rubes.
He jammed on his guitar and nearly blew out the coral tubes!
He was a brilliant creature who loved to take long walks.
He played rock music and even enjoyed intellectual talks.

This Saturday night, Rubes sang into the mic.
At the same time, Rita the Seahorse rode in on her bike.
Just when Rubes banged loudly on his guitar,
Rita was startled and her bike went flying far!

Before the band could stop,
Rita shot into the air,
her tail spun around
as she landed next to a chair.

Rita sat on the floor feeling a little dizzy,
her hair covered her face and got quite frizzy.
She felt embarrassed and had even injured her nose.
The whole restaurant was quiet—everyone froze.

Out from the kitchen, Izzy rushed to help.
Rubes dropped his guitar and made a bandage from sea kelp.
Rita felt better but was still a bit upset,
though Izzy and Rubes encouraged her not to fret.

Rubes walked up to the microphone and belted out a tune.
He dedicated it to Rita, and Izzy served her krill soup with a spoon.
The whole restaurant cheered and wished Rita well.
When Rubes finished playing, he gifted Izzy a special shell.

"My goodness," Izzy said, "what is this for?"
Rubes said, "Your kindness toward Rita warmed my heart to the core."
Izzy and Rubes bonded over the compassion they shared.
They became best friends—a very loving pair.

Questions for Discussion and Action in Practicing Kindness

1. What does kindness mean to you?

2. How do you show kindness to yourself?

3. How do you show kindness to others?

4. What are three things you can do to help someone else in need?

5. Can you think of a time you practiced kindness? How did it make you feel to be kind?

6. How does it make you feel when someone is kind toward you?

7. What are some kind things you can say to others?

8. If someone is hurt, how can you help them?

9. What makes someone a good friend?

10. It is special that we are all different! What are some things that make you different?

Being kind is awesome!

About the Author

Marlaina Mannella is a wife, mom, marketing professional, and writer. When she's not busy running her company, Marlaina can be found spending time with her enchanting and curious son, Palmer, her incredibly supportive husband, Nick, and their two silly French bulldogs, Biggie and Dumpling. She has always had a passion for writing and loves to create and tell stories on the spot, mostly inspired by her son and the world around them. Marlaina's debut children's book, *Izzy and Rubes Practice Kindness*, reflects her love of family, positive parenting, and the magic of childhood.

MarlainaM.com

@moonfoye